I was in big trouble.

"I need your help," I told Houdini. "It was my job to take care of Alfred. And now he's gone."

"I, the Great Houdini, will help you find him."

Houdini always tells me how great he is.

If he finds Alfred, I'll believe it.

First Stepping Stone Books you will enjoy:

By David A. Adler
(The Houdini Club Magic Mystery series)
Onion Sundaes
Wacky Jacks

By Kathleen Leverich
Brigid, Bewitched

By Mary Pope Osborne
(The Magic Tree House series)
Dinosaurs Before Dark (#1)
The Knight at Dawn (#2)
Mummies in the Morning (#3)
Pirates Past Noon (#4)

By Barbara Park
Junie B. Jones and the Stupid Smelly Bus
Junie B. Jones and a Little Monkey Business
Junie B. Jones and Her Big Fat Mouth
Junie B. Jones and Some Sneaky Peeky Spying

By Louis Sachar
Marvin Redpost: Kidnapped at Birth?
Marvin Redpost: Why Pick on Me?
Marvin Redpost: Is He a Girl?
Marvin Redpost: Alone in His Teacher's House

By Marjorie Weinman Sharmat
The Great Genghis Khan Look-Alike Contest
Genghis Khan: A Dog Star Is Born

By Camille Yarbrough
Tamika and the Wisdom Rings

A Houdini Club Magic Mystery

Wacky Jacks

by David A. Adler

illustrated by Heather Harms Maione

A FIRST STEPPING STONE BOOK

Random House New York

♥ *To Ariella, Dara, Natanya, and David*

Text copyright © 1994 by David A. Adler.
Illustrations copyright © 1994 by Heather Harms Maione.
"The Wacky Jack Trick" copyright © 1994 by Bob Friedhoffer.

Library of Congress Cataloging-in-Publication Data
Adler, David A. Wacky jacks / by David A. Adler ; illustrated by
 Heather Harms Maione. p. cm. — (A Houdini Club magic mystery)
"A First Stepping Stone book." SUMMARY: Janet and her cousin Herman
"Houdini" Foster investigate the mystery of their pet hamster's disappear-
ance from their classroom.
ISBN 0-679-84696-4 (trade) — ISBN 0-679-94696-9 (lib. bdg.)
[1. Schools—Fiction. 2. Hamsters—Fiction. 3. Lost and found
possessions—Fiction. 4. Mystery and detective stories.] I. Maione,
Heather Harms, ill. II. Title. III. Series: Adler, David A. Houdini Club
magic mystery.
PZ7.A2615Ham 1994 [E]—dc20 93-51259

Manufactured in the United States of America 10 9 8 7 6 5 4 3 2 1

Random House, Inc. New York, Toronto, London, Sydney, Auckland
A HOUDINI CLUB MAGIC MYSTERY is a trademark of Random House, Inc.

♣ Contents

♠ ♣ 1 ♥ ♦
The Wacky Jack Trick

Houdini was wearing his black cape and top hat. He was holding out the sides of his cape like they were wings. He looked funny, like he was going to fly off and bite someone's neck.

"Stand here," Houdini said.

I stood to the left of Houdini. He was about to do a magic trick.

I whispered to him, "People are watching."

We were in the hall at school. We were waiting for the morning bell to ring so we could go to class.

Houdini said, "Of course people are watching. Everyone wants to see the Great Houdini."

Houdini swirled his cape. "Come one! Come all! Watch the Great Houdini!"

A bunch of kids gathered around us. In the crowd were Dana, Rachel, and Tony from the Houdini Club.

Houdini started the Houdini Club a few months ago. We meet once a week in Dana's basement. Mostly, we watch Houdini do magic tricks. Usually, after he does a trick, he shows us how he did it.

Houdini smiled. He likes a crowd. He likes people to notice him.

Houdini took out a deck of cards and a

red bandanna. He covered the deck with the bandanna.

"My cousin, Janet Perry, will be my assistant," he said. Then he turned to me and said, "Cut the deck."

I reached under the bandanna and divided the deck in half.

"Herman Foster," Mr. Fish called out. "Are you causing trouble?"

Mr. Fish is the school principal.

Herman Foster is Houdini's real name. But Houdini doesn't like to be called Herman. He says that's too ordinary a name for him. He likes to be called Houdini, after Harry Houdini, who was once the world's greatest magician.

"Houdini isn't causing trouble," I told Mr. Fish. "He's just doing a magic trick."

Houdini pulled the bandanna off the

deck. "Take the top card," he told Mr. Fish.

Now Mr. Fish was Houdini's assistant!

I'm just an ordinary girl. I could never make the principal my assistant. But Houdini is almost a genius. That's why he gets away with lots of things.

Mr. Fish picked up the top card. It was

the Jack of Hearts.

"Now draw something wacky on it," Houdini told Mr. Fish. "Make it a Wacky Jack."

He gave Mr. Fish a black marker.

Mr. Fish drew a beard and eyeglasses on the Jack of Hearts.

"That's a Wacky Jack, all right," Rachel said.

Mr. Fish drew an open book. It looked like the Jack was reading.

"Reading is important," Mr. Fish told us.

"Now put the Wacky Jack back on the deck," said Houdini.

Mr. Fish put the card on top of the deck. Houdini straightened the cards.

RRRING!

The morning bell rang. It was time to go to class.

Houdini touched my shoulder. "Don't go anywhere," he said. "I am about to amaze you."

No one moved. Not even Mr. Fish.

Houdini took out his magic wand. He waved it over the cards.

"*Ala-kazam,* I am great. Yes, I am," he said.

Those are his magic words.

Houdini tapped the deck with the wand and gave it to Mr. Fish.

He said, "Now see if you can find the Wacky Jack."

Mr. Fish turned the cards over. He looked at every card. He even showed them to us.

The Wacky Jack was gone.

♥ ♣ 2 ♠ ♦
Alfred Is Gone!

"How did you do that?" Tony asked.

Houdini bowed and swirled his cape.

"I can make anything disappear," he said.

"That was a great trick," said Mr. Fish. "Now, please take off your hat and cape. I want you ready to learn."

Houdini took off his hat and cape and put them in his backpack.

Then he whispered to me, "I'll teach

you the trick after school, at our club meeting."

Houdini tapped me on my back and said, "Let's go."

We walked to class.

When we got to our room, Houdini and I hung up our jackets in the closet. We put our lunch bags on the shelf above our jackets.

I wanted to visit Alfred. He's our pet hamster. He lives in a tank with a screen on top. It's all the way in the back of the room. But our teacher Ms. Kane was there, talking to weird Mr. Morgan. Mr. Morgan was holding a small red box.

"Look in the back," I said to Houdini "Mr. Morgan is here."

Mr. Morgan is our science teacher. We

9

go to his room once a week for extra science. His room is really a laboratory, with test tubes, skeletons, and animals. Once he danced in class with one of the skeletons. He thought that was funny. We didn't.

I didn't know what Mr. Morgan was doing in our classroom. I hoped he wasn't going to tell us about the science fair again. I was tired of hearing about it.

"Hey, Houdini," said Tony. "Can you make Mr. Morgan disappear?"

Houdini took the magic wand out of his backpack. He pointed it at Mr. Morgan. Then he waved the wand in the air.

But he didn't say his magic words.

"Please be seated," Ms. Kane said.

Mr. Morgan didn't disappear. He was

still there. Houdini should have said his magic words.

"Don't forget about the science fair!" Mr. Morgan called out to us.

Then he went out the back door.

All the rooms at our school have two doors—a front and a back. We come in through the front door and leave through the back.

Ms. Kane checked to see who was here. Beverly, Jacob, and Mary Anne were absent.

"Please stand and recite the pledge to our flag."

It was Mr. Fish on the loudspeaker. He talks to the whole school every morning.

After the pledge Mr. Fish said, "Please be seated."

Mr. Fish told us about the science fair and the bake sale. Then he said, "Happy learning."

It was time to do our classroom jobs.

This week my job is to take care of Alfred. I feed him and give him water. On Friday I'll clean his tank.

In the beginning of the year, we all took turns taking care of Alfred. But then Simon forgot to put the screen on, and Alfred escaped. It took a long time to find Alfred and then catch him and put him back in the tank.

After that, Ms. Kane said a committee of just four people would take turns caring for Alfred. Jacob, Beverly, Dana, and I are on the committee. Jacob and Beverly have hamsters at home. And Ms. Kane said that

Dana and I are real responsible.

Houdini's job this week is to clean the erasers. He hates his job.

I took the bag of hamster food from Ms. Kane's closet.

"Look at the chalkboard," whispered Dana.

It's Simon's week to wash the board. He had drawn a large fish on it with the wet sponge. The fish was saying, "Happy learning."

Simon is always trying to do something funny.

"Hi, Alfred," I said as I came near his tank.

Of course, Alfred didn't answer. Hamsters don't talk to people.

Alfred was hiding this morning. I filled

his bowl with food. Then I looked for him.

Sometimes he hides behind his toy wheel. But he wasn't there.

And he wasn't behind his water bottle.

Or inside his tunnel.

Alfred was gone!

3

The Chalk Dust Ghost

Had Alfred escaped?

He couldn't have. I knew I had put the screen on the day before. It was on now.

Maybe Houdini made Alfred disappear. Maybe his magic wand missed Mr. Morgan and caught Alfred.

Houdini was in the front of the room. He looked like a ghost. His face and clothes were covered with chalk dust.

"Please finish your jobs and sit down," Ms. Kane said.

I put the bag of hamster food in Ms. Kane's closet. On the way to my seat, I passed Houdini. He was coughing.

"Alfred is gone," I said.

Houdini coughed.

"Did you make him disappear?" I asked.

Houdini coughed again.

"I hate chalk dust," he said.

Houdini clapped his hands together. Chalk dust flew off.

He slapped his clothes, waved his arms, and stamped his feet. Now Houdini

was standing in a cloud of chalk dust.
He quickly jumped aside, before the dust
landed on him again.

"Please be seated," Ms. Kane said.

She was teaching us about fractions. But I kept thinking about Alfred. The last time Alfred escaped, Ms. Kane yelled and screamed. Mostly at Simon. This time she would yell and scream at me.

I wrote a note.

Do you know where Alfred is? Did you make him disappear? From Janet.

Ms. Kane drew a large circle on the board. "Now imagine this is a pie," she said.

"What flavor pie?" Simon asked.

"It doesn't matter," Ms. Kane said.

"It matters to me," Simon told her. "I don't like apple pie."

I folded the note and wrote on the outside:

For Houdini.

I gave the note to Dana. She gave it to Jordan. He gave it to Rachel. She gave it to Houdini.

The door opened. It was Jacob. He wasn't absent. He was just late.

"Hang up your jacket and put your lunchbox away," Ms. Kane told Jacob.

Jacob sits right in front of me.

"Did I miss anything?" he asked me when he sat down.

"You missed Simon trying to be funny," I told him.

Ms. Kane drew a line through the large circle on the chalkboard. "Now we don't have one whole pie," she said. "We have two half pies."

"I don't have *any* pie," Simon said. "I have cookies in my lunch."

Ms. Kane looked at Simon. She sighed.

Then she said, "If you disrupt the lesson again, you will be sent to Mr. Fish."

Tuna fish or gold fish? I thought. That's what Simon always asks.

This time he didn't.

Simon's hands were in his desk. He had something in there. He was playing with it.

Dana poked me in my back. Then she dropped something on the floor. It was a note from Houdini.

It said:

. *I didn't make Alfred disappear. was the screen on?*

I looked at Houdini. I nodded my head.

What should I do, I wondered. Ms. Kane trusted me. She said I'm responsible. She'd be real angry when she found out that I lost Alfred. I'd probably have to clean the erasers every morning for the rest of the school year.

I had to find Alfred!

Dana poked me again. Then she pointed to Houdini.

His lips were moving. He was asking me something.

"Remind the meal?"

"What?" I asked.

"Unwind the seal?"

"What?"

Houdini wrote another note. He gave it to Rachel.

"Janet Perry, what fraction is each piece of the pie?" Ms. Kane asked.

I turned around. Ms. Kane had drawn another circle on the board. It had two lines through it.

"One fourth," I said.

I'm very good at math.

Dana dropped a note on the floor. I dropped my pencil. I bent down. I picked up the pencil and the note, too. I hid the note under my notebook.

Ms. Kane drew more circles on the board. She put lines through them. She shaded parts of each circle.

"Copy the pies," Ms. Kane said. "Then write what fraction is shaded."

Ms. Kane put the chalk down and began to walk around the room. She stopped by my desk. She stood there and watched me do the work.

I drew the first circle and the lines through it. I turned my notebook to do the shading. Houdini's note fell to the floor.

Ms. Kane picked it up.

Ms. Kane put the note in her pocket. She frowned at me. "I'll read this later," she said.

♥ ♣ 4 ♠ ♦
What a Day!

First I lost Alfred. Then Ms. Kane found my note.

What a day!

I did the math work.

Ms. Kane taught us a history lesson next.

I listened.

I even answered two questions.

"Close your books, please," Ms. Kane said.

It was time for recess.

I couldn't wait to get outside. I needed to talk to Houdini.

Ms. Kane had us line up one row at a time. She called Houdini's row first.

Houdini sits in the back of the room. He got up and went over to Alfred's tank. He looked inside. Then he walked to the closet, got his jacket, and went out into the hall.

My row was the last one called.

I wasn't the last one out of the room, though. Maria was right behind me. Then Jacob came out. He closed the door.

When I got into the hall, Houdini said, "In my note, the one Ms. Kane took, I asked if you had looked behind Alfred's wheel. But I looked and he's not there. He's gone."

"I know," I whispered. "And I'm in big trouble. I need your help."

He said, "Of course you need my help."

"It was my job to take care of Alfred," I said.

"I, the Great Houdini, will help you find him."

Houdini always tells me how great he is. If he finds Alfred, I'll believe it.

We went outside.

I said, "Maybe I should tell Ms. Kane."

Houdini shook his head. "No. First give me a chance to find Alfred."

He smiled.

"This is a mystery," he said as we walked. "And a mystery is like a magic trick. There's a logical explanation for every magic trick. And there's a logical explanation for every mystery."

We came to the monkey bars. No one else was playing on them.

I grabbed a rung and climbed to the

top. It didn't take me long. I'm good at
climbing.

"Alfred couldn't have escaped," I said.
"I put the screen on yesterday."

Houdini was taking his time going from one bar to the next. Finally he reached the top.

"I think someone took him," Houdini said.

"But who?" I asked. "Who would steal a hamster?"

Ms. Kane blew her whistle.

It was time to go back to class. Our class lined up.

Except for Simon. He was holding a big plastic spider. He was chasing a girl from another class. The girl was screaming.

"Maybe Simon took Alfred," Houdini said. "To play a practical joke."

Ms. Kane blew her whistle again.

Houdini and I went inside with the rest of the class.

After recess I didn't pay attention to the lesson. I watched Simon.

Simon listened to Ms. Kane. He wrote in his notebook. Then he reached into his desk.

Our desks have tops that lift up. Under the top is a cubby, for our books. Simon's hand was in his desk cubby. His hand was moving. He was playing with something.

Alfred!

5

I Know Who Took Alfred

"Close your books, please," Ms. Kane said.

It was time for lunch. Ms. Kane called us by rows to get our lunches.

My row was last again.

On my way to the closet, I stopped at Simon's desk. I lifted the top and peeked inside.

It was filled with tiny toy cars and junk food. But not Alfred. Simon must have been playing with the cars.

I went to the closet to get my lunch.

Then I ran into the hall to join the class.

There are benches and tables in the lunchroom. I sat between Houdini and Dana.

"Simon didn't take Alfred," I whispered. "He has toys and food in his desk. But no hamsters."

"Who wants to trade?" Rachel called out. "Who wants a cupcake?"

Houdini took out his dessert. A cup of lime pudding. He loves lime pudding.

Jacob had a slice of nut cake in his lunch bag.

Dana had potato chips.

Rachel and Dana traded.

I took out my cream cheese sandwich, bag of peanuts, and apple juice. I looked at them. Then I put them back in my lunch bag. I was too upset to eat.

"If Simon didn't take Alfred, who did?" Houdini mumbled. "I have to think about this."

He was talking to himself. He does that sometimes. No one heard him but me.

"What trick will Houdini teach us today?" Jordan asked.

He's in the Houdini Club, too.

"He'll teach us how to make a card disappear," Dana said.

I whispered to Dana, "Don't tell anyone, but Alfred is gone. Houdini is helping me find him."

"I'll just tell the other club members," Dana whispered back. "We can help you look for Alfred."

Houdini closed his eyes. He covered his ears. He thinks best when it's dark and quiet.

"Here comes Mr. Morgan," Rachel said. "Get ready to hear about the science fair again!"

Houdini's eyes were still closed.

Mr. Morgan is the teacher in charge of the lunchroom. I watched him walk from one table to the next.

Mr. Morgan came to our table. He asked us, "How are your science fair projects coming along?"

"Great!" Rachel said.

I didn't answer.

For my project I planted seeds in two pots. I watered one with soda and the other with water. Nothing grew. For the science fair, I'll just have two pots of dirt.

Houdini uncovered his ears and opened his eyes.

He looked at Mr. Morgan.

Houdini waited for Mr. Morgan to walk to another table. Then he turned to me and said, "I know who took Alfred!"

♥ ♣ 6 ♠ ♦

Skeletons and Snakes

After lunch we have to clear our tables. Then we can go outside to play. Houdini waited until everyone else at our table left.

Then he said, "Mr. Morgan was in our room this morning. He was standing right by Alfred's tank. He left carrying something in a red box. I think it was Alfred."

Mr. Morgan! I couldn't believe it.

"Why would he take Alfred?" I asked.

Houdini said, "Maybe he's using him for a science experiment. Mr. Morgan might be testing Alfred. To see how smart he is. Right now Alfred is probably trying to find his way through a maze."

Houdini thought for a moment. Then he said softly, "Or maybe Mr. Morgan is training Alfred with electric shocks."

"Electric shocks! Ouch!" I said. "No, I can't believe it."

Dana came back with Jordan, Melissa, Rachel, Daniel, Maria, and Tony. The whole Houdini Club!

"I told them about Alfred," Dana said.

"What should we do?" Maria asked.

Houdini looked around. Then he asked, "Where's Morgan?"

Rachel said, "He's outside."

"I think Mr. Morgan may have taken Alfred," Houdini said. "Janet and I will sneak into the science room. The rest of you watch Morgan. If he starts to walk inside, warn us. Tap on the window."

I cleared the table. Then Houdini and I left the lunchroom.

Mr. Morgan's room is near the lunchroom. Both doors were closed.

Houdini took a card from his pocket. It was the Wacky Jack! He hadn't made it disappear after all.

"Watch this," Houdini said. "With this card, I can unlock any door."

Houdini jiggled the card between the front door and the doorjamb.

I reached out and turned the knob. *Click!* The door wasn't locked.

Houdini tries to do things with tricks and magic. I'm just an ordinary girl. I turn doorknobs.

I opened the door, and we went into Mr. Morgan's room.

"Don't turn on the lights," Houdini whispered.

Mr. Morgan has lots of weird plants in his room. He feeds little bugs to one of them. He has tanks with spiders and fish and snakes in them. He has two birds in a large cage. The birds make a lot of noise.

On his desk are models of a heart and lungs, and a big eye. Behind his desk are two skeletons wearing jeans. Mr. Morgan thinks that putting jeans on the skeletons is funny. No one else does.

The shades were pulled almost all the way down. With the lights off, the skeletons

and the big eye were creepy. Wherever I went, I felt the eye was watching me.

I looked in one of the snake tanks.

"Maybe he fed Alfred to the snakes," Houdini whispered.

I thought about cute Alfred, his soft fur and his little tail.

"No," I said. "Even Mr. Morgan wouldn't do that."

I looked in the spider tank.

Spiders are not insects. They're arachnids. If you had a steel wire as thin as a spider's web, the spider's web would be stronger. I love spiders.

"Stop playing with the spiders," said Houdini. "Look for Alfred."

I checked the closet. Alfred wasn't there.

Then I saw the red box. It was on a table at the back of the room. It was the one Mr. Morgan had taken from our classroom.

I held it next to my ear. I didn't hear Alfred inside. Slowly I opened it.

It was filled with Popsicle sticks. Mr. Morgan probably needs them for the science fair.

"Look, Houdini!" I whispered. "Alfred's not in the red box."

Tap! Tap!

I turned. One of the birds was playing with the food dish.

Houdini was in the front of the room. He was looking in the bookcase.

Tap! Tap!

I looked at the birds again, but they weren't moving. Then I looked at the window. It was Dana. She was warning us.

There was someone at the front door.

♥ ♣ 7 ♠ ♦
I Had a Plan

The door opened. The lights went on.

I was hiding in the corner, right by the back door. I peeked out. I saw Mr. Morgan. He was writing on the chalkboard.

But where was Houdini?

He wasn't by the bookcase. I got down on my knees and looked around the room.

I found him.

Houdini was hiding behind one of the skeletons. Houdini saw me. He put his finger to his mouth. He wanted me to be quiet.

RRRING!

The bell rang.

I was right by the back door. It would be easy for me to get out of the room. But what about Houdini?

I had a plan.

I stood up. I opened the back door quietly and went out.

The hallway was crowded. Everybody was coming back from lunch and going to their classrooms. I walked to the front door of Mr. Morgan's room and knocked.

Mr. Morgan opened the door.

"Hello, Janet," he said.

I smiled.

"My family wants a pet," I said. "Mom

wants a cat, but I want a snake. What should we get?"

"Cats are good pets," he said. "They keep themselves very clean. Snakes are good pets, too. But some are dangerous."

I tried to look around Mr. Morgan, to see if Houdini had left the room. But I couldn't.

"Snakes are cold-blooded," Mr. Morgan said. "If you get a snake, you'll need to keep something warm in the tank."

"Hi, Janet."

I turned around. It was Houdini. He was standing in the hall behind me.

"Some people don't like snakes," Mr. Morgan said. "But a safe snake can make a very good pet."

I thanked Mr. Morgan, but he kept on talking. He was trying to be nice.

"We have to get to class," Houdini said.

Mr. Morgan smiled and told me, "We can talk about this later."

On our way to class, Houdini thanked me.

"You saved my life," he said. "I thought I would be stuck behind that skeleton forever."

Our class was having silent reading time. Everyone else was already reading. I quietly sat down and took out my book.

"Come with me, Janet. We need to talk."

It was Ms. Kane. She was standing right by my desk. I followed her out the back door.

"I'm surprised at you," Ms. Kane said. "You came back late from lunch."

I didn't say anything. I just looked down at the floor.

"And this morning you were passing notes."

The floor needed to be washed.

Ms. Kane took the note from her pocket. "What does this mean—Did you look behind the wheel?"

One of the floor tiles was broken.

"Janet, answer me. What's going on?"

I couldn't keep the secret any longer.

"Alfred is gone," I said.

Ms. Kane gasped. "Oh, no! Not again!"

She opened the door. I followed her into the room.

Everyone was reading. Houdini looked up from his book. He wanted to know if I was in trouble.

I followed Ms. Kane to Alfred's tank.

I pointed to the tank.

"See! Alfred is gone," I said.

Ms. Kane looked in the tank.

Then she said, "No, he's not."

I looked too.

Something was moving in Alfred's tank. It was small and furry.

Alfred was back!

♥ ♣ 8 ♠ ♦
A Real Mystery

I looked at Alfred.

Alfred looked at me.

He ran in a circle a few times. Then he stopped and looked at me again. He's so cute.

Ms. Kane said, "I don't understand your behavior at all, Janet. We'll discuss this after school."

I went back to my desk. I picked up my book. But I couldn't read it. The book was a mystery that some writer made up. I was trying to solve a *real* mystery.

Houdini said every mystery has a logical explanation. But nothing made sense. Why would someone steal Alfred and then return him?

Dana poked me in my back. There was a note on the floor. I looked at it. But I didn't pick it up.

Dana poked me again. I just kept pretending to be reading.

After silent reading, Ms. Kane taught us a grammar lesson. Something about nouns. But I didn't listen. I looked over at Houdini. He wasn't listening either.

Finally I heard Ms. Kane say, "Don't forget to do your homework. And study for your test tomorrow on fractions."

Class was over. It was time to get ready to go home.

I picked up the note. It was from Houdini. It said:

I saw something moving in Alfred's tank. Alfred is back.

I knew that.

We went to the closet one row at a time. My row was last, as usual.

When I got to the closet, Houdini was putting on his jacket. I put my jacket on, too. I picked up the bag with my left-over lunch.

Ms. Kane came over to me and said, "Please wait here, Janet. After I take the bus riders outside, I want to talk to you."

Houdini and I don't take the bus. We live near the school. We walk.

Houdini was by my seat, waiting with me. Jacob was in the back of the room. Maria was still getting her jacket. Everyone else was standing by the front door, waiting to leave.

RRRING!

The afternoon bell rang. It was time to go home. Everybody was leaving.

"Bus riders with me," said Ms. Kane. "Hurry up, Jacob."

"We're going ahead," Dana called to us. She was with the other Houdini Club members. "We'll set up the basement for the meeting. Don't be late."

Dana lives near the school too. We usually all walk together to Dana's house when the Houdini Club meets.

Houdini sat at the desk next to mine, looking at me. Then he looked at my lunch. He stared at it.

"It's my lunch," I said.

Houdini just kept staring at it.

"I couldn't eat it before. I was too upset," I said. "Maybe I'll eat it when I get home."

Houdini closed his eyes and covered his ears. He was thinking again.

I decided to visit Alfred. I went to the back of the room and looked in the tank.

I looked behind the water bottle.

I looked behind the wheel.

Alfred was gone again!

"Houdini!" I said. "You're not going to believe this!"

Houdini banged his fist on the desk. "I've got it! I know who took Alfred and put him back."

"And took him again," I said.

Houdini looked at me. I pointed to the tank.

Houdini jumped from his seat.

"Quick!" he said. "Stop the bus!"

9
Stop the Bus!

Did someone on the bus take Alfred?

I ran outside. Bus number six was just about to pull out. I ran past Ms. Kane. I waved my arms and shouted, "Stop the bus!"

The bus stopped. The door opened. I climbed inside.

"You have…to stop…the bus," I told the driver. I was out of breath.

"I just did," he said. "Now, please tell me *why* I stopped the bus."

I didn't know why.

I turned around and looked for Houdini. He was walking toward the bus. Ms. Kane and Mr. Fish were right behind him.

I waited.

"Well?" the bus driver asked.

Houdini got on the bus. Ms. Kane and Mr. Fish followed him up the steps.

"We have to see Jacob Winfield," said Houdini.

"Jacob Winfield," the driver called out.

"What's this all about?" Mr. Fish asked.

"Our pet hamster is missing, and Jacob has him," Houdini explained.

Jacob was coming down the aisle. He

heard Houdini accuse him of taking Alfred. He didn't deny it.

Houdini, Jacob, Ms. Kane, Mr. Fish, and I got off the bus. Then we went inside the school.

As we walked, I whispered to Houdini, "Jacob loves animals. He wouldn't steal Alfred. What makes you think he did?"

Houdini said, "It was your lunch bag that gave me the answer."

I opened my bag and looked inside. I wondered how a cream cheese sandwich, peanuts, and apple juice could help him solve a mystery.

When we got back to our classroom, Mr. Fish said, "Now, what's going on here?"

Houdini said, "Remember the Wacky Jack trick I did this morning? Well, I

didn't really make the card disappear.
When no one was looking, I moved it. I
put it where no one would think to look.
Especially you, Janet."

"Where was the Wacky Jack?" Mr. Fish
asked.

"That's a secret," Houdini said. "But I
will tell you how I found Alfred."

Houdini explained, "This morning
Jacob came late to class. Ms. Kane said—
hang up your jacket and put your
lunch*box* away. But in the lunchroom,
Jacob took his lunch out of his lunch *bag.*"

I asked, "Do you mean that when
Jacob came late to class, Alfred was in his
lunchbox?"

"Yes," Houdini answered. "And before
recess he was the last one out of the class.
That's when he put Alfred back in his

tank. Then, before he left to get on the bus, he took Alfred out again.

"Janet asked me to find Alfred, and I have. Right now Alfred is in Jacob's lunchbox."

Ms. Kane said, "Jacob, please open your lunchbox."

Jacob slowly opened it. There were tiny holes in the sides of the lunchbox. And wood shavings inside.

And there was Alfred! He looked up at all of us.

Jacob gently took Alfred out of the lunchbox.

"I didn't think Alfred was happy," Jacob explained. "A hamster needs friends."

Jacob put Alfred in his tank. He put the screen on the top.

"I have two hamsters at home," said Jacob. "I take Alfred home to play with them. I always put him back in his tank first thing in the morning. But today I was late."

We all watched Alfred. He was running in circles.

"He has such fun playing with Mandy and Morris," Jacob said. "Those are the names of my hamsters."

"We love Alfred, too," Ms. Kane said. "And we were worried about him. Janet felt responsible. She thought she had lost Alfred."

Ms. Kane told Jacob that if he wanted to take Alfred home, he should have asked her. Then she said that Alfred could visit with Mandy and Morris on weekends.

Ms. Kane said she would call Jacob's father. He could come to school and take Jacob home.

"And now," Mr. Fish said to Houdini, "would you like to tell me how you made that card disappear?"

"The Great Houdini will never tell," Houdini said. "Except to other magicians."

Other magicians!

I looked at my watch.

"Oh my!" I said. "We have a club meeting and we're late. We're always late!"

♥ ♣ 10 ♠ ♦
Ala-kazam!

We hurried to Dana's house. When we got there, the whole club was on the front porch. Waiting for us.

"You're late," said Dana. "You're always late."

"I'm worth waiting for," Houdini said as he walked into the house.

We all followed Houdini down to the basement.

"Did you find Alfred?" Jordan asked.

"Yes!" I said. I told everyone all about Alfred and Jacob, and Mandy and Morris.

While I talked, Houdini went into the laundry room. That's where he prepares his magic tricks.

"Was Ms. Kane mad?" Tony asked.

"No, she was real nice," I answered. "She even said Jacob could take Alfred home on weekends."

"Look here, ladies and gentlemen!" Houdini called as he came out of the laundry room. "I, the Great Houdini, am about to mystify and amaze you."

He was wearing his cape and hat. He had a red bandanna in his pocket.

Houdini bowed. He smiled. It was one of his big magic show smiles. I could see his back teeth.

"Maria, will you please assist me."

Maria stood next to Houdini. She bowed and smiled, too.

Houdini showed us a deck of cards. Then he took the red bandanna from his pocket and covered the deck.

"Now, reach under the bandanna and cut the deck," Houdini told Maria.

She did.

Houdini took off the bandanna. He told Maria to show everyone the top card.

It was the Jack of Clubs.

When Mr. Fish cut the deck, the top card was the Jack of Hearts. When Maria cut the deck, the top card was the Jack of Clubs! How did Houdini make everybody pick a Jack?

"Draw something wacky on the card," Houdini said. "Make it a Wacky Jack."

Maria drew a curly mustache and an eye patch.

She put the card back on top of the deck.

"Stand back," Houdini told Maria. He took Maria's shoulder and moved her out of the way. "I want to make sure everyone can see the magic."

Suddenly I remembered something Houdini did this morning, when I saw the trick for the first time. Now I knew just where he put the Wacky Jack!

Houdini took out his magic wand and waved it over the deck. "*Ala-kazam*. I am great. Yes, I am," he said.

Yes, Houdini *is* great. He found Alfred!

"Now find the Wacky Jack," Houdini told Maria. He gave the deck to her. She looked at every card. The Wacky Jack was gone.

"Wow!" said Daniel.

Houdini took a bow.

Then Houdini put his arm around Maria's shoulder. They bowed together.

"Now," Houdini said, "I'll teach you the trick." And he did.

The Wacky Jack Trick
♣ by Bob Friedhoffer ♠

EFFECT:

A card, chosen and marked by a volunteer, vanishes from the deck.

PROPS: A bandanna

A deck of cards

Clear tape

PREPARATION:

- Put the bandanna in your pocket.
- Make a small loop (about 1/2" in diameter) with the tape, sticky side out. Stick the loop to your belt or waistband.
- Take a Jack from the deck of cards and put it *face down* on the top of the deck, just like all the other cards.
- Take another card (let's say, the Five of Hearts). Put it *face up* on the bottom of the deck.
- Turn the deck of cards over. Now the Five of Hearts is the top card. Since the Five of Hearts is face down, it will look as if all the cards are face down. Put the deck back in the box.

69

ROUTINE AND PATTER:

"I will now perform my world-famous Wacky Jack Trick."

• Take the deck out of the box and hold it in your left hand. The audience will see the back of the Five of Hearts on top, and think the deck is face down.

• Take the bandanna from your pocket and shake it open. Lay the bandanna over the deck of cards in your left hand.

"May I have a volunteer from the audience, please?"

• Ask the volunteer to *cut the deck* underneath the bandanna. The volunteer will reach beneath the bandanna and take half the cards off the top of the deck.

• After the volunteer does this, turn the half of the deck that is still in your left hand over. No one will see you do this, since your hand is beneath the bandanna.

• The Jack is now on top of your half of

70

the deck, face down. Remove the bandanna and drop it on the table. Hold your half of the deck out to the volunteer.

"Thank you. Now will you please turn over the card you cut to? I have a funny feeling it might be a Jack."

• The volunteer turns over the top card. The volunteer and the audience will be surprised that, as you predicted, the card is a Jack.

• NOTE: You have just done what magicians call "forcing a card." You have "forced" the volunteer to pick the card you wanted him or her to pick. This is a useful technique for many card tricks.

"Well, it's a Jack all right. But it's not wacky yet. Please draw something wacky on the Jack with this marker."

• While the audience watches the volunteer draw on the Jack, take back the other half of the cards and turn over the Five of

Hearts so all the cards are facing the same direction. Put the whole deck back together and hold it in your left hand. Then reach down and put the middle finger of your right hand through the loop of tape on your belt.

"Put the Wacky Jack back on top of the deck, please."

• After the volunteer puts the card back on top of the deck, bring your right hand to the deck as if you are straightening it and let the loop of tape stick to the back of the Wacky Jack. Meanwhile, ask the volunteer to move off to your left side so everyone can see you finish the trick.

• As the volunteer moves to your left side, drop your right hand (be careful to leave the loop of tape on the card!) and reach your left hand (with the deck still in it) to the volunteer's back. Touch the volunteer with your left hand for just a moment, as if you are showing him or her where to stand. At this point the Wacky Jack, with the tape on it, should stick to the volunteer's back.

• Bring your left hand, with the deck, back to the front of your body.

"I am now going to make your Wacky Jack disappear from the deck!"

• Make some mysterious motions over the deck with your right hand or a magic wand. Then say some magic words, such as "abracadabra." You might also want to riffle the cards for dramatic effect.

• Hand the deck to the volunteer and ask him or her to find the Wacky Jack. The volunteer will be amazed to find that the card has vanished!

• NOTE: After the trick is over, put your arm around the volunteer's back and ask him or her to take a bow with you. While your hand is crossing the volunteer's back, remove the card.

About the Authors

DAVID ADLER was one of six children in his family. "I used to do magic tricks to get attention," he says. "Now I write books to get attention!"

David has written many books for kids, including the acclaimed *Cam Jansen* series. He lives in Woodmere, New York, with his wife and their three sons.

BOB FRIEDHOFFER, known as the "Madman of Magic," created the Wacky Jack Trick. Bob has been a magician for over fifteen years, and has even performed at the White House. He currently lives and works in New York City.